Dedicated to all those who believe

in magic and fairy tales.

This book belongs to:

_____

(your name here)

Always believe
in magic!

Dave
Busto

ISBN: 0-9975027-1-1

ISBN-13: 978-0-9975027-1-8

Published by Gooberly Press

Pick Me! Pick Me!

The Story of the Magic Pumpkin

Written by:

Dave Bastien

Illustrated by:

Patrick Riley

They went to buy a pumpkin
In the patch on Old Mack's farm

And the farmer said, "While you look,
Just hold this magic charm."

"Then close your eyes and hold it tight
And you'll hear one speak to you.
So please, don't pick just any one –
Whatever you may do!"

So they went into the patch
For what seemed so ever long

Watching, waiting, 'til they heard
What seemed a little song.

The words were kind of muffled, like
From a mouth that's full of seeds
But when they got much closer
They could hear them all with ease!

"Pick me! Pick me!" they heard one say,
"I've heard the stories told
Of children's laughter, ghouls and ghosts
Way back from days of old."

"And I'd gladly give up all my seeds
For a single day of life,
And let you make a happy face
With your little pocket knife!"

Much to their surprise, they said,
"The farmer, he was right!
This will be the pumpkin
That will be with us tonight!"

So they gave it eyes and a crooked smile
And watched its life transform,
With a great big candle for its heart
To keep it ever warm.

They set it on the stairs
Where the children came to call,
And lit the candle set inside
So it smiled at one and all.

Vampires, ghosts and monsters too!
They all came and went

And the pumpkin smiled happily
When the night was finally spent.

It said, "I never thought I'd see this day
And I thank you from my heart,
Please leave me here 'til morning
And then I'll have to part.

'Cause a magic pumpkin lives
For this single magic day,
And of all my seeds there's only one
That can grow again this way."

"So plant them all and feed them love
And we may meet again.
Now close my lid and let me sleep
And keep the warmth within."

So they went to bed with happy hearts
And dreamed their wish came true.
And the life they gave the pumpkin
Now lives on in me and you!

"Pick me! Pick me!" they heard one say,
"I've heard the stories told
Of children's laughter, ghouls and ghosts
Way back from days of old."

"And I'd gladly give up all my seeds
For a single day of life,
And let you make a happy face
With your little pocket knife!"

CPSIA information can be obtained
at www.ICGtesting.com
Printed in the USA
BVOW05s0232220917

495082BV00001B/1/P